BIG EYES, SCARY VOICE

Edel Wignell
illustrated by Carl Pearce

Tamarind

One evening,
in the park
at sunset,
Tania and Josh
hear a voice,
a scary voice,
hooting,
"Who? Who?"

They walk
through the park
towards the voice...

Whoo?
Whoo?

... to the fountain.

They stand and
stare at the big eyes,
and listen
for the scary voice.
But there is no voice,
just the sound
of water falling,
swishing, swirling.

They wait and listen once more. The voice hoots, "Who? Who?"

Tania and Josh leave the fountain and walk across the grass towards the scary voice.

Soon they reach…

... the playground, where everything is still: *swings and slides, monkey bars and climbing net.*

They walk on, towards...

... the magic boat.

They stand and
stare at the big eyes
and listen.
But no-one is there.
Everything is still
and quiet.

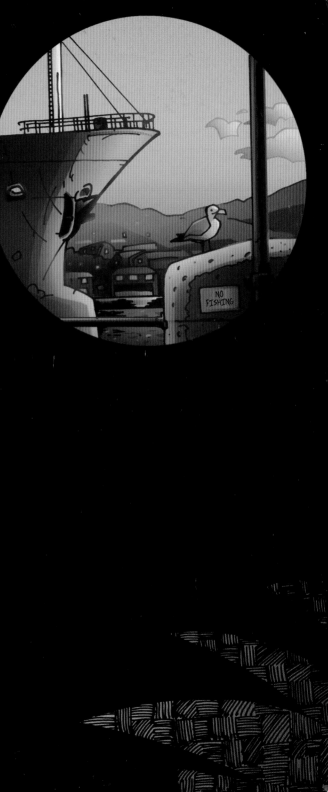

Once again
the scary voice
drifts across
from the trees,
louder now,
nearer.
"Who? Who?"
Closer now,
much closer.

Tania and Josh listen,
then they leave
the boat and walk
across the grass
towards the voice
in the trees.

In one of the trees
there is a hollow.
In the hollow sits
a feathery thing
with big eyes and
a scary voice.
It hoots twice,
"Who? Who?"

W hoo?

W hoo?

Hearts thumping,
Tania and Josh race back to Mum.
"There's something in a tree…" shouts Josh.
"A feathery thing!"

"A feathery thing, with big eyes and a scary voice," shouts Tania.
"Come and see," says Josh.

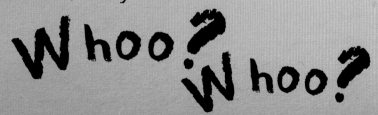

They hurry back.

There sits the feathery thing,
with the big eyes and
the scary voice.

For Ainslie – E.W.
To Em, Mum & Dad, Cornwall and Noir – C.P.

Big Eyes, Scary Voice
TAMARIND BOOKS 978 1 870 51688 4

Published in Great Britain by Tamarind Books,
a division of Random House Children's Books
A Random House Group Company

This edition published 2008

1 3 5 7 9 10 8 6 4 2

Text Copyright © Edel Wignell, 2008
Illustrations copyright © Carl Pearce, 2008

Set in Mirarae BT

TAMARIND BOOKS
61–63 Uxbridge Road, London, W5 5SA

www.tamarindbooks.co.uk
www.kidsatrandomhouse.co.uk
www.rbooks.co.uk

Addresses for companies within The Random House Group Limited can be found at:
www.randomhouse.co.uk/offices.htm

THE RANDOM HOUSE GROUP Limited Reg. No. 954009

A CIP catalogue record for this book is available from the British Library.

Printed and bound in China

Other Tamarind titles available:

FOR READERS OF
Big Eyes and Scary Voice

The Night the Lights Went Out
Choices, choices…
What Will I Be?
South African Animals
Caribbean Animals
All My Friends
A Safe Place
Dave and the Tooth Fairy
Where's Gran?
Time for Bed
Time to Get Up
Giant Hiccups

FOR TODDLERS

The Best Blanket
The Best Home
The Best Mum
The Best Toy

Let's Feed the Ducks
Let's Go to Bed
Let's Have Fun
Let's Go to Playgroup

I Don't Eat Toothpaste Anymore
Are We There Yet?

BOOKS FOR WHEN YOU GET A LITTLE OLDER…

The Dragon Kite
Princess Katrina and the Hair Charmer
The Feather
The Bush
Mum's Late
Marty Monster
Starlight
Dizzy's Walk
Boots for a Bridesmaid
Yohance and the Dinosaurs

FOR BABIES

Baby Goes
Baby Plays
Baby Noises
Baby Finds

AND IF YOU ARE INTERESTED IN
SEEING THE REST OF OUR LIST,
PLEASE VISIT OUR WEBSITE:
www.tamarindbooks.co.uk